LEAVE YOUR SLEEP

A collection of classic children's poetry
adapted to music by

NATALIE MERCHANT

and illustrated by

BARBARA McCLINTOCK

FRANCES FOSTER BOOKS

Farrar Straus Giroux
New York

To Lucía, with all my love
—N.M.

With thanks to Kevin Donohue,
Frances Foster, Jennie Dunham,
Roberta Pressel, and David Johnson
—B.M.

CONTENTS

Girls and boys, come out to play,
　　The moon doth shine as bright as day;
Leave your supper, and leave your sleep,
　　And come with your playfellows into the street.
　　　　　　　　　　　　　　—Mother Goose

INTRODUCTION

This collection of songs represents the long conversation I had with my daughter during the first six years of her life. It documents our word-of-mouth tradition in the poems, stories, and songs that I found to delight and teach her—this parade of witches and fearless girls, blind men and elephants, giants and sailors and gypsies, dancing bears, circus ponies, a Chinese princess and a janitor's boy. I tried to show her that speech could be the most delightful toy in her possession and that her mother tongue is rich with musical rhythms and rhymes. With these poems, I gave her parables with lessons on human nature and bits of nonsense to challenge the natural order of things and sharpen her wit. Poetry speaks of so much: longing and sadness, joy and beauty, hope and disillusionment. These are the things that make a childhood, that time when we wake up to the great wonders and small terrors of our world. Poets are our soft-spoken clairvoyants. But poetry on the page can be difficult to penetrate; sometimes it needs to be heard. I used music to enter these poems, and once inside I was able to understand how they were constructed with layers of feeling and meaning.

Five years of research and writing went into *Leave Your Sleep*. It was the most ambitious project I had ever attempted, and the process consumed me. As I adapted their poems to music, my curiosity about the lives of these poets grew. So I read biographical accounts and letters, searched archives, and contacted heirs, executors, or the poets themselves in an attempt to know more. The research and writing accounted for only a portion of the labor and love put into the project. I collaborated with more than a hundred talented musicians and a small, dedicated team of recording technicians over the course of a full year to realize my vision for this album.

When Frances Foster contacted me with the plan to transform this collection of songs into a picture book for children, I was intrigued. But when she suggested that Barbara McClintock be the illustrator, I was thrilled. Her work has delighted and charmed me for many years; it is of the greatest technical quality yet deeply soulful. I've always had a love for picture books; their illustrations, poems, and stories create and preserve a place of innocence we move through as children but can return to as adults. My hope is that this collaborative book of poems, pictures and music will provide many enchanted hours to children eager for beauty and the sort of adventure that happens between the pages of a book and the words of a song.

—*Natalie Merchant*

THE LAND OF NOD

Robert Louis Stevenson (1850–1894)

From breakfast on all through the day
At home among my friends I stay;
But every night I go abroad
Afar into the land of Nod.

All by myself I have to go,
With none to tell me what to do—
All alone beside the streams
And up the mountain-sides of dreams.

The strangest things are there for me,
Both things to eat and things to see,
And many frightening sights abroad
Till morning in the land of Nod.

Try as I like to find the way,
I never can get back by day,
Nor can remember plain and clear
The curious music that I hear.

THE DANCING BEAR

ALBERT BIGELOW PAINE (1861–1937)

Oh, it's fiddle-de-dum and fiddle-de-dee,

The dancing bear ran away with me;

For the organ-grinder he came to town

With a jolly old bear in a coat of brown.

And the funny old chap joined hands with me,

While I cut a caper and so did he.

Then 'twas fiddle-de-dum and fiddle-de-dee,

I looked at him, and he winked at me,

And I whispered a word in his shaggy ear,

And I said, "I will go with you, my dear."

Then the dancing bear he smiled and said,
Well, he didn't say much, but he nodded his head,
As the organ-grinder began to play
"Over the hills and far away."
With a fiddle-de-dum and a fiddle-de-dee,
Oh, I looked at him and he winked at me,
And my heart was light and the day was fair,
And away I went with the dancing bear.

Oh, 'tis fiddle-de-dum and fiddle-de-dee,
The dancing bear came back with me;
For the sugar-plum trees were stripped and bare,
And we couldn't find cookies anywhere.
And the solemn old fellow he sighed and said,
Well, he didn't say much, but he shook his head,
While I looked at him and he blinked at me
Till I shed a tear and so did he;
And both of us thought of our supper that lay
Over the hills and far away.

Then the dancing bear he took my hand,
And we hurried away through the twilight land;
And 'twas fiddle-de-dum and fiddle-de-dee
When the dancing bear came back with me.

THE JANITOR'S BOY

Nathalia Crane (1913–1998)

Oh I'm in love with the janitor's boy,
    And the janitor's boy loves me;
He's going to hunt for a desert isle
    In our geography.

A desert isle with spicy trees
    Somewhere near Sheepshead Bay;
A right nice place, just fit for two
    Where we can live alway.

Oh I'm in love with the janitor's boy,
    He's busy as he can be;
And down in the cellar he's making a raft
    Out of an old settee.

He'll carry me off, I know that he will,
    For his hair is exceedingly red;
And the only thing that occurs to me
    Is to dutifully shiver in bed.

The day that we sail, I shall leave this brief note,
    For my parents I hate to annoy:
"I have flown away to an isle in the bay
    With the janitor's red-haired boy."

ADVENTURES OF ISABEL

Ogden Nash (1902–1971)

Isabel met an enormous bear,
Isabel, Isabel, didn't care;
The bear was hungry, the bear was ravenous,
The bear's big mouth was cruel and cavernous.
The bear said, Isabel, glad to meet you,
How do, Isabel, now I'll eat you!
Isabel, Isabel, didn't worry,
Isabel didn't scream or scurry.
She washed her hands and she straightened her hair up,
Then Isabel quietly ate the bear up.

Once in a night as black as pitch
Isabel met a wicked old witch.
The witch's face was cross and wrinkled,
The witch's gums with teeth were sprinkled.
Ho, ho, Isabel! the old witch crowed,
I'll turn you into an ugly toad!
Isabel, Isabel, didn't worry,
Isabel didn't scream or scurry.
She showed no rage and she showed no rancor,
But she turned the witch into milk and drank her.

Isabel met a hideous giant,
Isabel continued self-reliant.
The giant was hairy, the giant was horrid,
He had one eye in the middle of his forehead.
Good morning, Isabel, the giant said,
I'll grind your bones to make my bread.
Isabel, Isabel, didn't worry,
Isabel didn't scream or scurry.
She nibbled the zwieback that she always fed off,
And when it was gone, she cut the giant's head off.

Isabel met a troublesome doctor,
He punched and he poked till he really shocked her.
The doctor's talk was of coughs and chills
And the doctor's satchel bulged with pills.
The doctor said unto Isabel,
Swallow this, it will make you well.
Isabel, Isabel, didn't worry,
Isabel didn't scream or scurry.
She took those pills from the pill concocter,
And Isabel calmly cured the doctor.

BLEEZER'S ICE-CREAM

JACK PRELUTSKY (1940–   )

I am Ebenezer Bleezer,
I run BLEEZER'S ICE-CREAM STORE,
there are flavors in my freezer
you have never seen before,
twenty-eight divine creations
too delicious to resist,
why not do yourself a favor,
try the flavors on my list:

COCOA MOCHA MACARONI
TAPIOCA SMOKED BOLONEY
CHECKERBERRY CHEDDAR CHEW
CHICKEN CHERRY HONEYDEW
TUTTI-FRUTTI STEWED TOMATO
TUNA TACO BAKED POTATO
LOBSTER LITCHI LIMA BEAN
MOZZARELLA MANGOSTEEN
ALMOND HAM MERINGUE SALAMI
YAM ANCHOVY PRUNE PASTRAMI
SASSAFRAS SOUVLAKI HASH
SUKIYAKI SUCCOTASH

BUTTER BRICKLE PEPPER PICKLE
POMEGRANATE PUMPERNICKEL
PEACH PIMENTO PIZZA PLUM
PEANUT PUMPKIN BUBBLEGUM
AVOCADO BRUSSELS SPROUT
PERIWINKLE SAUERKRAUT
BROCCOLI BANANA BLUSTER
CHOCOLATE CHOP SUEY CLUSTER
COTTON CANDY CARROT CUSTARD
CAULIFLOWER COLA MUSTARD
ONION DUMPLING DOUBLE DIP
TURNIP TRUFFLE TRIPLE FLIP
GARLIC GUMBO GRAVY GUAVA
LENTIL LEMON LIVER LAVA
ORANGE OLIVE BAGEL BEET
WATERMELON WAFFLE WHEAT

I am Ebenezer Bleezer,
I run BLEEZER'S ICE-CREAM STORE,
taste a flavor from my freezer,
you will surely ask for more,
twenty-eight divine creations
too delicious to resist,
come on, do yourself a favor,
try the flavors on my list.

15

OLD MOTHER HUBBARD & HER DOG REVISITED

JOHN YEOMAN (1934–)

Said Old Mother Hubbard, one dark winter's night,
While giving a bath to her goat,
"That dog looks like he's been having a fight;
I wish he'd take pride in his coat."

The very next morning she had a great shock
Which made her feel weak at the knees,
For there was the dog, wearing beret and smock,
Painting pictures of birds in the trees.

He went indoors, leaving his paintings to dry;
She followed—and what do you think?
He was dressed as a sailor, a patch on one eye,
With a small fleet of boats in the sink.

Said Old Mother Hubbard, "You're getting me down;
Oh, won't you behave yourself, please?"
But five minutes later, got up like a clown,
He was juggling pieces of cheese.

So Old Mother Hubbard lay down to relax;
She felt a slight ache in her head.
But dressed as a burglar, with crowbar and axe,
The dog stole the legs of the bed.

Then Old Mother Hubbard heard no noise at all.
Now, did that mean mischief or not?
She found him downstairs, dressed in bonnet and shawl,
And gurgling away in his cot.

"Oh, do something useful!" the poor woman cried.
The dog scratched his head thinking hard.
Then, in helmet and armor, he clattered outside,
Giving chase to the mice in the yard.

Thought Old Mother Hubbard, while bolting the door,
"He's so disobedient and rude!
But I won't pass remarks on his coat anymore;
He's better behaved in the nude."

THE BLIND MEN AND THE ELEPHANT

JOHN GODFREY SAXE (1816–1887)

It was six men of Indostan
    To learning much inclined,
Who went to see the Elephant
    (Though all of them were blind),
That each by observation
    Might satisfy his mind.

The *First* approached the Elephant,
    And happening to fall
Against his broad and sturdy side,
    At once began to bawl:
"God bless me! but the Elephant
    Is very like a wall!"

The *Second*, feeling of the tusk,
    Cried, "Ho! what have we here
So very round and smooth and sharp?
    To me 'tis mighty clear
This wonder of an Elephant
    Is very like a spear!"

The *Third* approached the animal,
    And happening to take
The squirming trunk within his hands,
    Thus boldly up and spake:
"I see," quoth he, "the Elephant
    Is very like a snake!"

The *Fourth* reached out an eager hand,
    And felt about the knee.
"What most this wondrous beast is like
    Is mighty plain," quoth he;
"'Tis clear enough the Elephant
    Is very like a tree!"

The *Fifth* who chanced to touch the ear,
    Said: "E'en the blindest man
Can tell what this resembles most;
    Deny the fact who can,
This marvel of an Elephant
    Is very like a fan!"

The *Sixth* no sooner had begun
    About the beast to grope,
Than, seizing on the swinging tail
    That fell within his scope,
"I see," quoth he, "the Elephant
    Is very like a rope!"

And so these men of Indostan
    Disputed loud and long,
Each in his opinion
    Exceeding stiff and strong,
Though each was partly in the right,
    And all were in the wrong!

Moral

So oft in theologic wars,
    The disputants, I ween,
Rail on in utter ignorance
    Of what each other mean,
And prate about an Elephant
    Not one of them has seen!

TOPSYTURVEY-WORLD

William Brighty Rands (1823–1882)

If the butterfly courted the bee,
  And the owl the porcupine;
If churches were built in the sea,
  And three times one was nine;
If the pony rode his master,
  If the buttercups ate the cows,
If the cat had the dire disaster
  To be worried by the mouse;
If Mama sold the baby
  To a gypsy for half a crown;
If a gentleman was a lady—
  The world would be Upside-Down!
If any or all of these wonders
  Should ever come about,
I should not consider them blunders,
  For I should be Inside-Out!

IT MAKES A CHANGE

Mervyn Peake (1911–1968)

There's nothing makes a Greenland whale
Feel half so high and mighty
As sitting on a mantelpiece
In Aunty Mabel's nighty.
It makes a change from Freezing Seas
(Of which a whale can tire),
To warm his weary tail at ease
Before an English fire.
For this delight he leaves the seas
(Unknown to Aunty Mabel),
Returning only when the dawn
Lights up the Breakfast Table.

THE PEPPERY MAN

ARTHUR MACY (1842–1904)

The Peppery Man was cross and thin;
He scolded out and scolded in;
He shook his fist, his hair he tore;
He stamped his feet and slammed the door.

Heigh ho, the Peppery Man,
The rabid, crabbed Peppery Man!
Oh, never since the world began
Was any one like the Peppery Man.

His ugly temper was so sour
He often scolded for an hour;
He gnashed his teeth and stormed and scowled,
He snapped and snarled and yelled and howled.

He wore a fierce and savage frown;
He scolded up and scolded down;
He scolded over field and glen,
And then he scolded back again.

His neighbors, when they heard his roars,
Closed their blinds and locked their doors,
Shut their windows, sought their beds,
Stopped their ears and covered their heads.

He fretted, chafed, and boiled and fumed;
With fiery rage he was consumed,
And no one knew, when he was vexed,
What in the world would happen next.

Heigh ho, the Peppery Man,
The rabid, crabbed Peppery Man!
Oh, never since the world began
Was any one like the Peppery Man.

CALICO PIE

EDWARD LEAR (1812–1888)

Calico Pie,
    The little Birds fly
Down to the calico tree,
    Their wings were blue
    And they sang "Tilly-loo!"
    Till away they flew,—
And they never came back to me!
    They never came back!
    They never came back!
They never came back to me!

Calico Jam,
    The little Fish swam,
Over the syllabub sea,
    He took off his hat,
    To the Sole and the Sprat,
    And the Willeby-Wat,—
But he never came back to me!
    He never came back!
    He never came back!
He never came back to me!

Calico Ban,
    The little Mice ran,
To be ready in time for tea,
    Flippity flup,
    They drank it all up,
    And danced in the cup,—
But they never came back to me!
    They never came back!
    They never came back!
They never came back to me!

Calico Drum,
    The Grasshoppers come,
The Butterfly, Beetle, and Bee,
    Over the ground,
    Around and around,
    With a hop and a bound,—
But they never came back to me!
    They never came back!
    They never came back!
They never came back to me!

IF NO ONE EVER MARRIES ME

LAURENCE ALMA-TADEMA (1865–1940)

If no one ever marries me—
    And I don't see why they should,
For nurse says I'm not pretty,
    And I'm seldom very good—

If no one ever marries me
    I shan't mind very much;
I shall buy a squirrel in a cage,
    And a little rabbit-hutch.

I shall have a cottage near a wood,
    And a pony all my own,
And a little lamb quite clean and tame,
    That I can take to town.

And when I'm getting really old—
    At twenty-eight or -nine—
I shall buy a little orphan-girl
    And bring her up as mine.

EQUESTRIENNE

RACHEL FIELD (1894–1942)

See, they are clearing the sawdust course
For the girl in pink on the milk-white horse.

Her spangles twinkle; his pale flanks shine,
Every hair of his tail is fine

And bright as a comet's; his mane blows free,
And she points a toe and bends a knee,

And while his hoofbeats fall like rain
Over and over and over again.

And nothing that moves on land or sea
Will seem so beautiful to me

As the girl in pink on the milk-white horse
Cantering over the sawdust course.

THE SLEEPY GIANT

CHARLES EDWARD CARRYL (1841–1920)

My age is three hundred and seventy-two,
    And I think, with the deepest regret,
How I used to pick up and voraciously chew
    The dear little boys whom I met.

I've eaten them raw, in their holiday suits;
    I've eaten them curried with rice;
I've eaten them baked, in their jackets and boots,
    And found them exceedingly nice.

But now that my jaws are too weak for such fare,
    I think it exceedingly rude
To do such a thing, when I'm quite well aware
    Little boys do not like to be chewed.

And so I contentedly live upon eels,
    And try to do nothing amiss,
And I pass all the time I can spare from my meals
    In innocent slumber—like this.

NURSERY RHYME OF INNOCENCE AND EXPERIENCE

CHARLES CAUSLEY (1917–2003)

I had a silver penny
    And an apricot tree
And I said to the sailor
    On the white quay

"Sailor O sailor
    Will you bring me
If I give you my penny
    And my apricot tree

"A fez from Algeria
    An Arab drum to beat
A little gilt sword
    And a parakeet?"

And he smiled and he kissed me
    As strong as death
And I saw his red tongue
    And I felt his sweet breath

"You may keep your penny
    And your apricot tree
And I'll bring your presents
    Back from sea."

O the ship dipped down
    On the rim of the sky
And I waited while three
    Long summers went by

Then one steel morning
    On the white quay
I saw a grey ship
    Come in from sea

Slowly she came
    Across the bay
For her flashing rigging
    Was shot away

All round her wake
    The seabirds cried
And flew in and out
    Of the hole in her side

Slowly she came
    In the path of the sun
And I heard the sound
    Of a distant gun

And a stranger came running
   Up to me
From the deck of the ship
   And he said, said he

"O are you the boy
   Who would wait on the quay
With the silver penny
   And the apricot tree?

"I've a plum-coloured fez
   And a drum for thee
And a sword and a parakeet
   From over the sea."

"O where is the sailor
   With bold red hair?
And what is that volley
   On the bright air?

"O where are the other
   Girls and boys?
And why have you brought me
   Children's toys?"

maggie and milly
and molly and may

E. E. Cummings (1894–1962)

maggie and milly and molly and may
went down to the beach (to play one day)

and maggie discovered a shell that sang
so sweetly she couldn't remember her troubles, and

milly befriended a stranded star
whose rays five languid fingers were;

and molly was chased by a horrible thing
which raced sideways while blowing bubbles, and

may came home with a smooth round stone
as small as a world and as large as alone.

For whatever we lose (like a you or a me)
it's always ourselves we find in the sea

THE KING OF CHINA'S DAUGHTER

(ANONYMOUS)

The king of China's daughter
    So beautiful to see
With her face like yellow water,
    Left her nutmeg tree.

Her little rope for skipping
    She kissed and gave it me
Made of painted notes of singing-birds
    Among the fields of tea.

I skipped across the nutmeg grove
    I skipped across the sea;
But neither sun nor moon, my dear,
    Has yet caught me.

VAIN AND CARELESS

ROBERT GRAVES (1895–1985)

Lady, lovely lady,
    Careless and gay!
Once, when a beggar called,
    She gave her child away.

The beggar took the baby,
    Wrapped it in a shawl—
"Bring her back," the lady said,
    "Next time you call."

Hard by lived a vain man,
    So vain and so proud
He would walk on stilts
    To be seen by the crowd,

Up above the chimney pots,
    Tall as a mast—
And all the people ran about
    Shouting till he passed.

"A splendid match surely,"
    Neighbours saw it plain,
"Although she is so careless,
    Although he is so vain."

But the lady played bobcherry,
    Did not see or care,
As the vain man went by her,
    Aloft in the air.

This gentle-born couple
    Lived and died apart—
Water will not mix with oil,
    Nor vain with careless heart.

I SAW A SHIP A-SAILING

(Anonymous)

I saw a ship a-sailing,
    A-sailing on the sea;
And it was full of pretty things
    For baby and for me.

There were sweetmeats in the cabin,
    And apples in the hold;
The sails were made of silk,
    And the masts were made of gold.

The four-and-twenty sailors
    That stood between the decks,
Were four-and-twenty white mice,
    With chains about their necks.

The captain was a duck,
    With a packet on his back;
And when the ship began to move,
    The captain cried, "Alas, alack!"

I saw a ship a-sailing,
    A-sailing on the sea;
And it was full of pretty things
    For baby and for me.

THE POETS

ROBERT LOUIS STEVENSON
"The Land of Nod"

ALBERT BIGELOW PAINE
"The Dancing Bear"

NATHALIA CRANE
"The Janitor's Boy"

OGDEN NASH
"Adventures of Isabel"

JACK PRELUTSKY
"Bleezer's Ice-Cream"

JOHN YEOMAN
"Old Mother Hubbard
& Her Dog Revisited"

JOHN GODFREY SAXE
"The Blind Men
and the Elephant"

WILLIAM BRIGHTY RANDS
"Topsyturvey-World"

MERVYN PEAKE
"It Makes a Change"

ARTHUR MACY
"The Peppery Man"

EDWARD LEAR
"Calico Pie"

LAURENCE ALMA-TADEMA
"If No One Ever Marries Me"

RACHEL FIELD
"Equestrienne"

CHARLES EDWARD CARRYL
"The Sleepy Giant"

CHARLES CAUSLEY
"Nursery Rhyme of
Innocence and Experience"

E. E. CUMMINGS
"maggie and milly and
molly and may"

ROBERT GRAVES
"Vain and Careless"

CREDITS AND PERMISSIONS

The Land of Nod

Robert Louis Stevenson photograph by Charles L. Ritzmann from the Henry W. and Albert A. Berg Collection of English and American Literature, the New York Public Library, Astor, Lenox and Tilden Foundations.

The Dancing Bear

Albert Bigelow Paine photograph courtesy of the Mark Twain Project, the Bancroft Library, University of California, Berkeley (ABP 1906).

The Janitor's Boy

"The Janitor's Boy," written by Nathalia Crane © 1924 Nathalia Crane. Used with permission of estate.

Nathalia Crane photograph courtesy of Brooklyn Public Library.

Adventures of Isabel

"Adventures of Isabel," by Ogden Nash, used by permission of Curtis Brown, Ltd., copyright © 1936, all rights reserved.

Ogden Nash photograph courtesy of Getty Images.

Bleezer's Ice-Cream

Text from the poem "Bleezer's Ice-Cream" in *The New Kid on the Block*, text copyright © 1984 by Jack Prelutsky, used by permission of HarperCollins Publishers.

Photograph of Jack Prelutsky used with permission of Jack Prelutsky.

Old Mother Hubbard & Her Dog Revisited by John Yeoman,
"Old Mother ᵘᵗᵈ· ᵇᵃʳᵈ &ᵃˡᴵ of John Yeoman. Used by from AP ⁿ
permiₛ∙ᵖʰ of John Yeoman courtesy of Mike White.
Pʰ

he Blind Men and the Elephant

John Godfrey Saxe photograph by Mathew Brady from the Library of Congress, Prints & Photographs Division (LC-DIG-cwpbh-01888).

Topsyturvey-World

William Brighty Rands photograph courtesy of David Rands.

It Makes a Change

"It Makes a Change," written by Mervyn Peake. Used with permission of estate.

Mervyn Peake photograph (© Sebastian Peake, 2009) is reproduced by permission of PFD (www.pfd.co.uk) on behalf of the Estate of Mervyn Peake.

The Peppery Man

Arthur Macy photograph courtesy of the Nantucket Historical Association (P7201).

Calico Pie

Edward Lear photograph from Houghton Library, Harvard University (MS Typ 55.10).

If No One Ever Marries Me

Laurence Alma-Tadema photograph (with her father) © National Portrait Gallery, London.

Equestrienne

Rachel Field photograph by Ben Pinchot from the Schlesinger Library, Radcliffe Institute, Harvard University.

The Sleepy Giant

Charles Edward Carryl photograph courtesy of New York Stock Exchange Archives, NYSE Euronext.

Nursery Rhyme of Innocence and Experience

"Nursery Rhymᵉ ᵒf ᴵⁿⁿᵒᶜᵉˡⁿᶜᵉ and Eₓperience," written by ᴴᵃʳˡ᫂ ᴄ ᵤsley. Used with permission of estate.

Charles Causley photograph courtesy of Special Collections, University of Exeter and the Estate of Charles Causley.

maggie and milly and molly and may

"maggie and milly and molly and may," written by E. E. Cummings © 1956, 1984, 1991 by the Trustees for the E. E. Cummings Trust, from *Complete Poems: 1904–1962*, edited by George J. Firmage. Used by permission of Liveright Publishing Corporation.

E. E. Cummings photograph by Edward Weston © 1981 Center for Creative Photography, Arizona Board of Regents.

Vain and Careless

"Vain and Careless," by Robert Graves, from *Complete Poems in One Volume*, used by permission of Carcanet.

Robert Graves photograph from AP Watt Ltd. on behalf of the Trustees of the Robert Graves Copyright Trust.

MUSIC CREDITS

The Land of Nod
Sean O'Loughlin & Natalie Merchant, *orchestration*; Sandra Park, *violin*; Sharon Yamada, *violin*; Lisa Kim, *violin*; Ann Lehmann, *violin*; Arnaud Sussmann, *violin*; Minyoung Baik, *violin*; Shan Jiang, *violin*; Matt Lehmann, *violin*; Robert Rinehart, *viola*; Karen Dreyfus, *viola*; Eileen Moon, *cello*; Jeanne LeBlanc, *cello*; Jeremy McCoy, *bass*; Sherry Sylar, *oboe*; Marc Goldberg, *bassoon*; Lino Gomez, *bass clarinet*; Phil Myers, *French horn*; Michelle Baker, *French horn*; Erik Ralske, *French horn*; Howard Wall, *French horn*; Mike Davis, *tenor trombone*; Birch Johnson, *tenor trombone*; George Flynn, *bass trombone*; Kyle Turner, *tuba*; Erik Charlston, *percussion*; Ina Zdorovetchi, *harp*.

The Dancing Bear
The Klezmatics (Richie Barshay, *frame drum, poyk, snare drum*; Lorin Sklamberg, *accordion*; Paul Morrisset, *acoustic bass guitar, baritone horn*; Matt Darriau, *alto saxophone, clarinet, bass clarinet*; Frank London, *trumpet, alto horn*; Lisa Gutkin, *fiddle*; the Klezmatics, *gang vocals*).

The Janitor's Boy
Wynton Marsalis, *arrangement, trumpet*; Daniel Nimmer, *piano*; Ali Jackson, *drums*; Walter Blanding, *saxophone*; Carlos Henriquez, *bass*; Doug Wamble, *banjo, guitar*; Victor Goines, *clarinet*; Wycliffe Gordon, *trombone*; the Ditty Bops (Abby DeWald, *vocals*; Amanda Barrett, *vocals*). (Wynton Marsalis appears courtesy of the Orchard. Victor Goines appears courtesy of Rosemary Joseph Records. Wycliffe Gordon appears courtesy of Bluesback Records.)

Adventures of Isabel
Gabriel Gordon, *guitar*; Judy Hyman, *fiddle*; Richard Stearns, *banjo*; Mark Murphy, *upright bass*; Blake Miller, *accordion*.

Bleezer's Ice-Cream
Wynton Marsalis, *arrangement, trumpet*; Daniel Nimmer, *piano*; Ali Jackson, *drums*; Walter Blanding, *saxophone*; Carlos Henriquez, *bass*; Doug Wamble, *guitar*; the Fairfield Four (Isaac Freeman, *vocals*; Edward Hall, *vocals*; Robert Hamlett, *vocals*; Joe Rice, *vocals*; Joseph Thompson, *vocals*). (Wynton Marsalis appears courtesy of the Orchard.)

Old Mother Hubbard & Her Dog Revisited
Sean O'Loughlin, *string arrangement*; Sandra Park, *violin*; Sharon Yamada, *violin*; Robert Rinehart, *viola*; Eileen Moon, *cello*; Jeremy McCoy, *bass*; Sherry Sylar, *oboe*; Marc Goldberg, *bassoon*; Lino Gomez, *bass clarinet*.

The Blind Men and the Elephant
Hazmat Modine (Rich Huntley, *drums*; Pete Smith, *banjo*; Steve Elson, *clarinet, baritone saxophone*; Pam Fleming, *trumpet*; Michael Gomez, *lap steel*; Wade Schuman, *diatonic harmonica*; William Barrett, *chromatic harmonica*; Joseph Daley, *tuba*); the Fairfield Four (Isaac Freeman, *vocals*; Edward Hall, *vocals*; Robert Hamlett, *vocals*; Joe Rice, *vocals*; Joseph Thompson, *vocals*); the Ditty Bops (Abby DeWald, *vocals*; Amanda Barrett, *vocals*). (Hazmat Modine appears courtesy of Barbès Records.)

Topsyturvey-World
Clark Gayton, *horn arrangement, trombone*; Horace James, *keyboards*; Hoova Simpson, *bass*; Andrew Bassford, *guitar*; Larry McDonald, *percussion*; Paul Sutton, *drums*; Gerald Johnson, *saxophone*; Eddie Allen, *trumpet*; Joanne Williams, *vocals*; Kimberly Miller, *vocals*. (Clark Gayton appears courtesy of Ritual Ltd.)

It Makes a Change
Medeski Martin & Wood (John Medeski, *piano*; Billy Martin, *drums*; Chris Wood, *bass*); Michael Leonhart, *horn arrangement, trumpet*; Dan Levine, *bass trombone, tuba, alto horn*; Dieter Hennings, *acoustic guitar*; Katell Keineg, *vocals*. (Michael Leonhart appears courtesy of Sunnyside Records.)

The Peppery Man
Hazmat Modine (Rich Huntley, *drums*; Pete Smith, *electric guitar*; Steve Elson, *baritone saxophone, B-flat clarinet*; Pam Fleming, *trumpet*; Michael Gomez, *dobro*; Wade Schuman, *diatonic harmonica*; William Barrett, *chromatic harmonica*; Joseph Daley, *tuba*); the Fairfield Four (Isaac Freeman, *vocals*; Edward Hall, *vocals*; Robert Hamlett, *vocals*; Joe Rice, *vocals*; Joseph Thompson, *vocals*). (Hazmat Modine appears courtesy of Barbès Records.)

Calico Pie
Gabriel Gordon, *guitar*; Judy Hyman, *fiddle*; Richard Stearns, *banjo*; Mark Murphy, *upright bass*; Bill Spence, *hammer dulcimer*.

If No One Ever Marries Me
Gabriel Gordon, *guitar*; Richard Stearns, *banjo*; Mark Murphy, *upright bass*; Bill Spence, *hammer dulcimer*.

Equestrienne
Stephen Barber & Natalie Merchant, *orchestration*; Meridian Arts Ensemble (Jon Nelson, *trumpet*; Daniel Grabois, *horn*; Benjamin Herrington, *trombone*; Brian McWhorter, *trumpet*; Raymond Stewart, *tuba*); Sandra Park, *violin*; Sharon Yamada, *violin*; Karen Dreyfus, *viola*; Eileen Moon, *cello*; Artis Wodehouse, *pump organ*; Greg Cohen, *bass*. (Meridian Arts Ensemble appears courtesy of Channel Classical Records and Eight Ball Records.)

The Sleepy Giant
Natalie Merchant, *arrangement*; John Roberts, *concertina, voice of the manservant*; Dieter Hennings, *baroque guitar, theorbo*; Motomi Igarashi, *viola da gamba*; Deidre Rodman, *harpsichord*; Nina Stern, *recorder, chalumeau*.

Nursery Rhyme of Innocence and Experience
Sean O'Loughlin & Natalie Merchant, *string arrangement*; Lúnasa (Trevor Hutchinson, *upright bass*; Kevin Crawford, *low whistle*; Paul Meehan, *acoustic guitar*; Cillian Vallely, *uilleann pipes*; Sean Smyth, *fiddle*); Sandra Park, *violin*; Sharon Yamada, *violin*; Lisa Kim, *violin*; Ann Lehmann, *violin*; Arnaud Sussmann, *violin*; Minyoung Baik, *violin*; Shan Jiang, *violin*; Matt Lehmann, *violin*; Robert Rinehart, *viola*; Karen Dreyfus, *viola*; Eileen Moon, *cello*; Jeanne LeBlanc, *cello*; Jeremy McCoy, *bass*.

maggie and milly and molly and may
Stephen Barber, *string arrangement*; Erik Della Penna, *guitar*; Marc Friedman, *bass*; Sterling Campbell, *drums*; Sandra Park, *violin*; Sharon Yamada, *violin*; Karen Dreyfus, *viola*; Eileen Moon, *cello*.

The King of China's Daughter
Natalie Merchant & Stephen Barber, *arrangement*; Wang Guo Wei, *erhu*; Weng Po Wei, *dizi flute*; Sun Li, *pipa*; Sandra Park, *violin*; Sharon Yamada, *violin*; Karen Dreyfus, *viola*; Eileen Moon, *cello*; Katell Keineg, *vocals*.

Vain and Careless
Natalie Merchant, *arrangement*; Dieter Hennings, *lute*; Nina Stern, *recorder*; Motomi Igarashi, *viola da gamba*.

I Saw a Ship A-Sailing
Lúnasa (Trevor Hutchinson, *upright bass*; Kevin Crawford, *low whistle*; Paul Meehan, *acoustic guitar*; Cillian Vallely, *low whistle*).

Produced by Natalie Merchant and Andres Levin
Recording Engineer: Nick Wollage
Assistant Engineer: Eli Walker
Recording Studio: The Clubhouse, Rhinebeck, NY
(Second Assistant Engineer: Dustin Wicksell)
Additional recording at Avatar Studios, New York, NY (Assistant Engineer: Rick Kwan); Legacy Recording Studios, New York, NY (Assistant Engineers: Angie Teo, Derik Lee & Peter Wolford); and the Sound Kitchen, Nashville, TN (Engineer: Nick Brophy; Assistant Engineer: Adam Deane)
Mix Engineer: Steve Rosenthal
Mix Studio: The Magic Shop (Second Assistant Engineers: Brian Thorn & Kabir Hermon)
Mastering Engineer: Robert C. Ludwig
Mastering Studio: Gateway Mastering Studios
Project Coordinators: Sue Berger & Megan Ingalls
Photo Researcher / Licensing Coordinator: Sarah Cullen
Photo Restoration: Sebastian Wintermute

ACKNOWLEDGMENTS

I would like to acknowledge my family, friends, and colleagues for all their help and encouragement throughout this project. My gratitude to all the poets for their wonderful poems and to their descendants, publishers, and literary executors for their invaluable help. —N.M.

My thanks to Natalie Merchant for her passion, vision, and brilliant virtuosity in creating this amazing musical extension of well-considered poems. —B.M.

Permissions to reprint poems and author photographs are found on the credits and permissions page.

Farrar Straus Giroux Books for Young Readers
175 Fifth Avenue, New York 10010

Copyright © 2012 by Natalie Merchant
Pictures copyright © 2012 by Barbara McClintock
All rights reserved
Distributed in Canada by D&M Publishers, Inc.
Color separations by Embassy Graphics
Printed in China by South China Printing Co. Ltd.,
Dongguan City, Guangdong Province
Designed by Roberta Pressel and Natalie Merchant
First edition, 2012
1   3   5   7   9   10   8   6   4   2

mackids.com

Library of Congress Cataloging-in-Publication Data
Leave your sleep / [selected by] Natalie Merchant ; pictures by Barbara McClintock.
— 1st ed.
    p.   cm.
ISBN 978-0-374-34368-2 (hardcover)
1. Poetry—Collections.   I. Merchant, Natalie.   II. McClintock, Barbara, ill.
PN6101.L43 2012
808.81'99282—dc23
                                                    2011047064